PERFECT PETUNIAS

Lynn Jenkins

illustrated by Kirrili Lonergan

EK

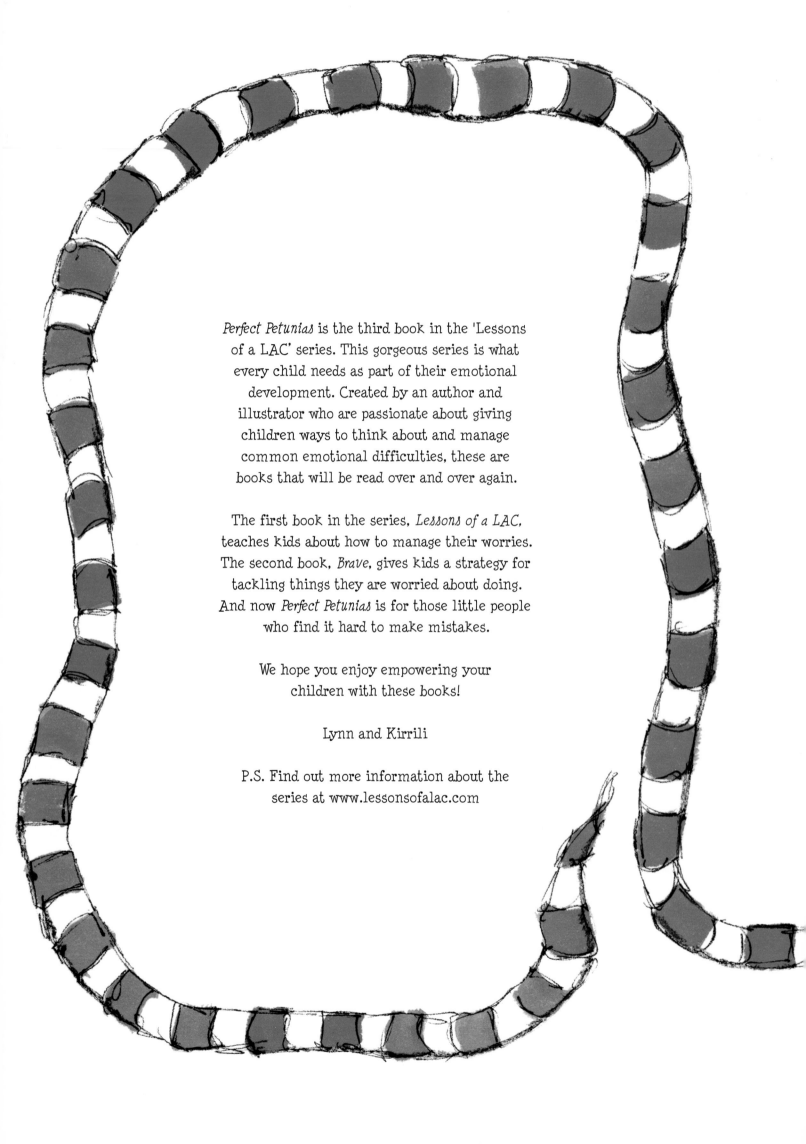

Perfect Petunias is the third book in the 'Lessons of a LAC' series. This gorgeous series is what every child needs as part of their emotional development. Created by an author and illustrator who are passionate about giving children ways to think about and manage common emotional difficulties, these are books that will be read over and over again.

The first book in the series, *Lessons of a LAC*, teaches kids about how to manage their worries. The second book, *Brave*, gives kids a strategy for tackling things they are worried about doing. And now *Perfect Petunias* is for those little people who find it hard to make mistakes.

We hope you enjoy empowering your children with these books!

Lynn and Kirrili

P.S. Find out more information about the series at www.lessonsofalac.com

In a little hut in a little village
on the very top of a mountain,
Loppy Lac and Curly Calmster
were doing their homework.

Loppy was practising writing
the letter 'a'.

Suddenly, he threw down his pencil.
'OK, that's it! I'm starting again!

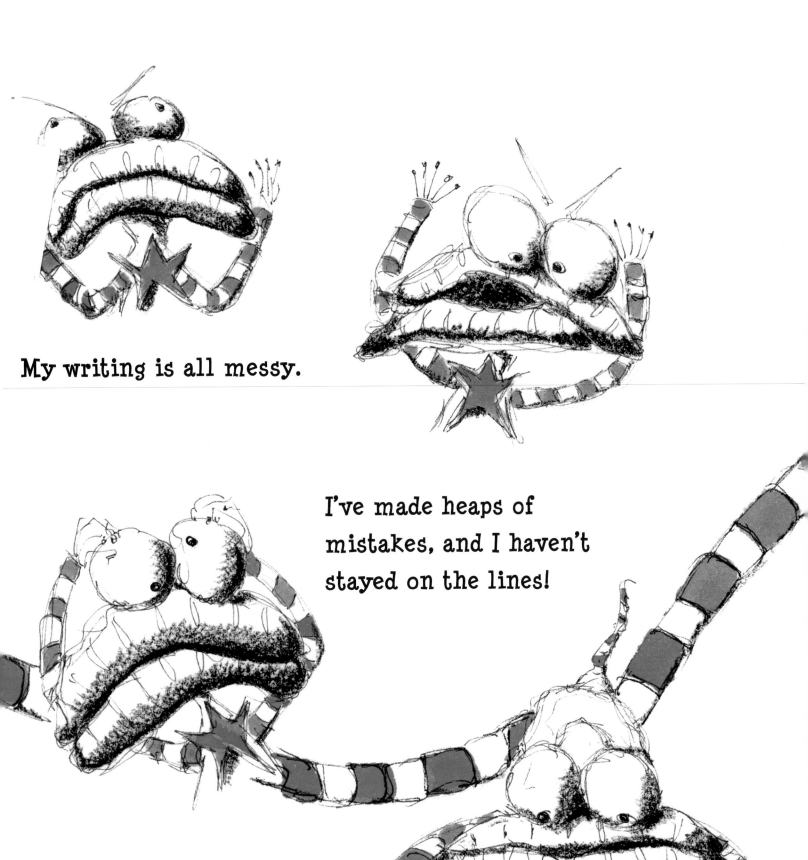

My writing is all messy.

I've made heaps of
mistakes, and I haven't
stayed on the lines!

I'm hopeless!'

And he stomped off.

'I can't do anything right!'

he yelled, as he slammed the door.

sed his eyebrows.
Loppy's trying to
ct petunias again.'

He sighed and walked
to the door. 'I'll be
out in the garden,' he
called. 'Come out when
you're ready, Loppy.'

Curly waited for Loppy
to join him in the
garden. He waited ...

and waited . . .

and waited.

The sun was just starting
to think about going to
bed for the night, when
Curly heard Loppy's feet
flip-flopping towards him.

'I'm not really in the mood for gardening, Curly,' said Loppy grumpily.

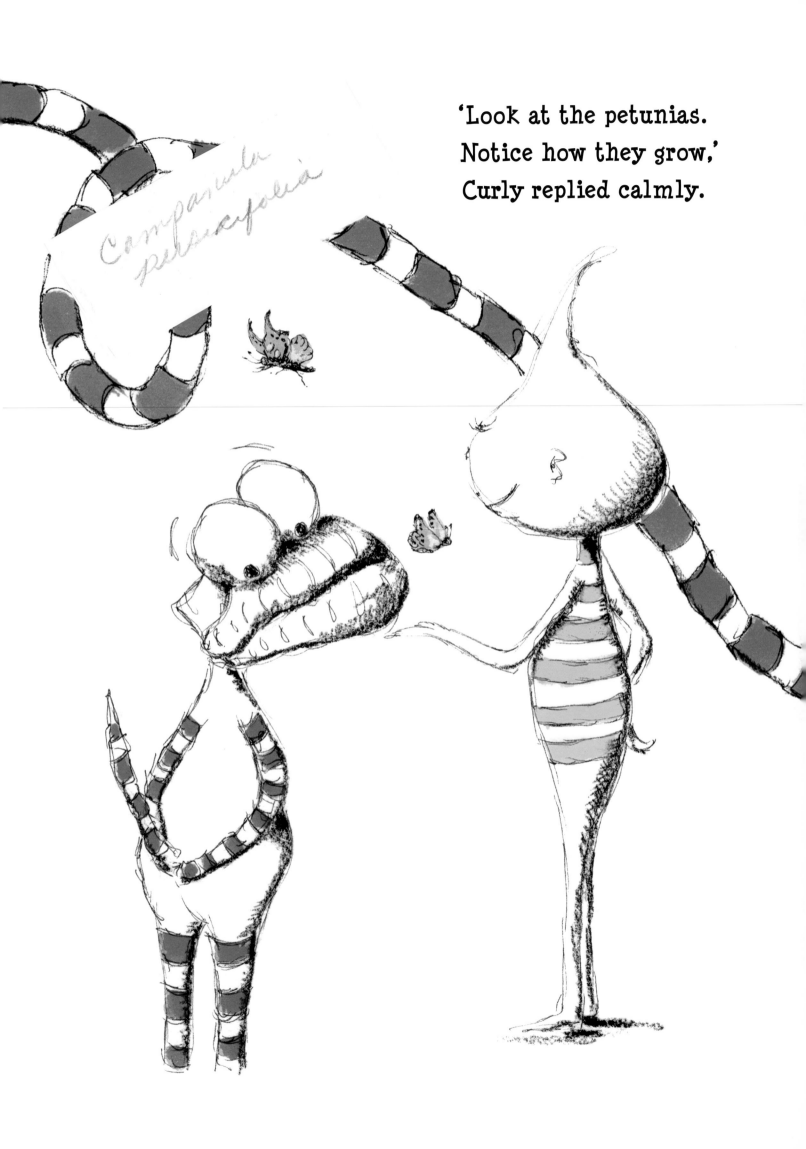

'Look at the petunias.
Notice how they grow,'
Curly replied calmly.

Loppy looked. 'They grow
all over the place.'

'Exactly,' Curly continued.
'We plant them, water them,
let them be. And then they grow
how they grow. Petunias grow
in all different directions. We
can't control the way they grow.'

'When you try to control everything you do, Loppy,
it's like you're trying to control the way petunias grow.'

'I don't try to control everything!' snapped Loppy.

'Well, just now you were trying to control not making mistakes and not being messy. Being OK with how you do things is all part of letting your petunias grow how they grow.'

'I was trying to do my best,' said Loppy, feeling confused. 'I thought it was always important to try my best.'

'Yes, you're right. It is important to always try your best and THAT is success, Loppy – TRYING your best.

When you truly focus on the "trying"
part you are being the most perfect YOU.'

Curly touched a petunia. 'Think back
to when you planted these petunias.
What did you focus on the most?'

Loppy remembered. He thought that
he hadn't dug them in deep enough ...

hadn't spaced them out properly ...

and hadn't put enough water on them.

'I focused most on my
mistakes,' Loppy said quietly.

'If you focus on your mistakes,
Loppy, that's all you'll see. And look
what you miss out on,' said Curly.

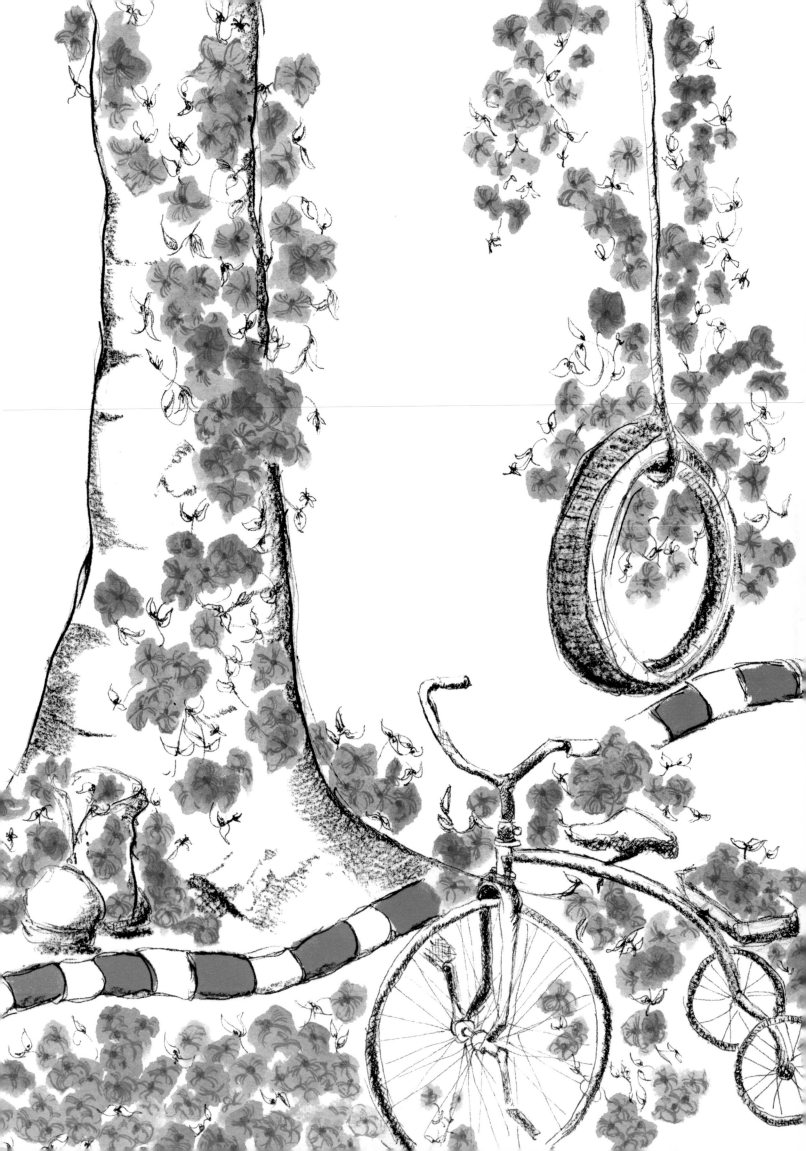

They sat in silence for a moment. Loppy thought hard about what Curly had said.

Then Loppy stood up, picked a petunia
and walked towards the house.

'I'm going to do my homework,' he told Curly. 'I'm taking this petunia to remind me that I just need to let things be sometimes. I can do what I can, then I need to let my petunias grow.'

And Loppy was excited
to see what would
happen when he did!

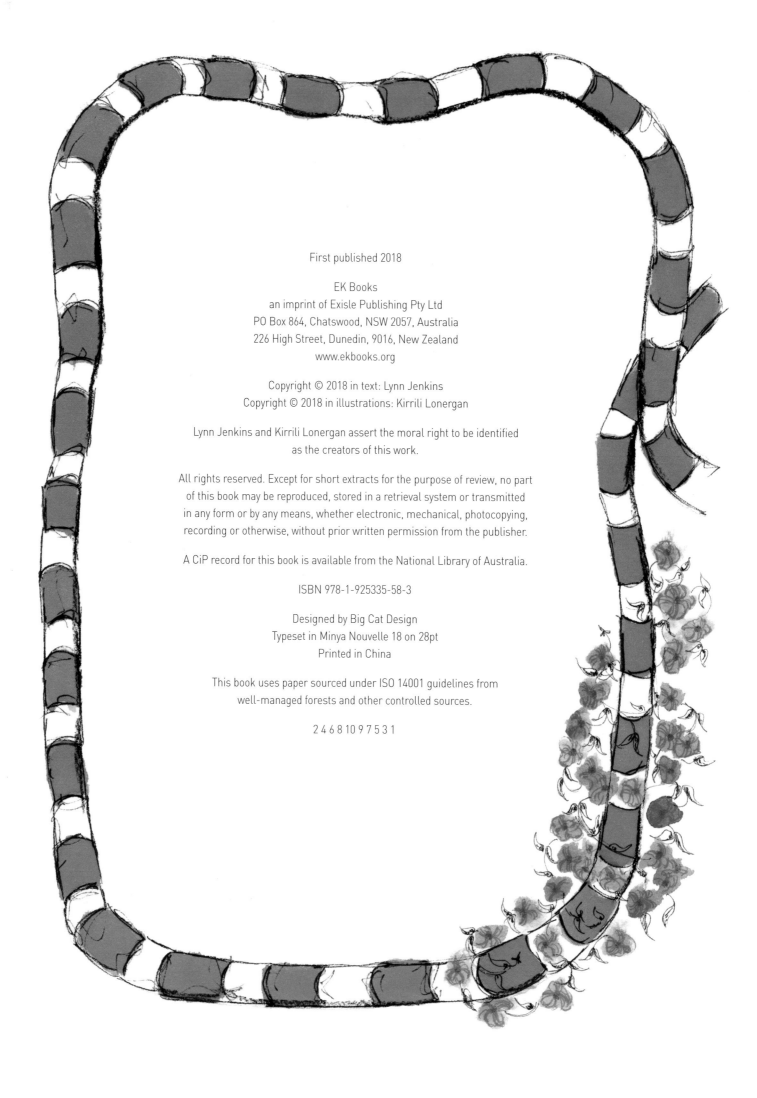

First published 2018

EK Books
an imprint of Exisle Publishing Pty Ltd
PO Box 864, Chatswood, NSW 2057, Australia
226 High Street, Dunedin, 9016, New Zealand
www.ekbooks.org

A CiP record for this book is available from the National Library of Australia.

ISBN 978-1-925335-58-3

Designed by Big Cat Design
Typeset in Minya Nouvelle 18 on 28pt
Printed in China

This book uses paper sourced under ISO 14001 guidelines from
well-managed forests and other controlled sources.

2 4 6 8 10 9 7 5 3 1